SALTY

Based on *The Railway Series* by the Rev. W. Awdry

Illustrations by
Robin Davies and Creative Design

EGMONT

EGMONT

We bring stories to life

First published in Great Britain in 2004
by Egmont UK Limited
239 Kensington High Street, London W8 6SA
This edition published in 2008

Thomas the Tank Engine & Friends™

CREATED BY BRITT ALLCROFT

HiT entertainment

ISBN 978 1 4052 3465 8

1 3 5 7 9 10 8 6 4 2

Printed in Italy

The Forest Stewardship Council (FSC) is an international, non-governmental organisation
dedicated to promoting responsible management of the world's forests. FSC operates a
system of forest certification and product labelling that allows consumers to identify
wood and wood-based products from well managed forests.

For more information about Egmont's paper buying policy please visit www.egmont.co.uk/ethicalpublishing

For more information about the FSC please visit their website at www.fsc.uk.org

This is a story about Salty the Dockyard Diesel. He loved working by the sea, so he didn't think he would like it when I sent him to work at the Quarry. But as it turned out, he was very good with the trucks …

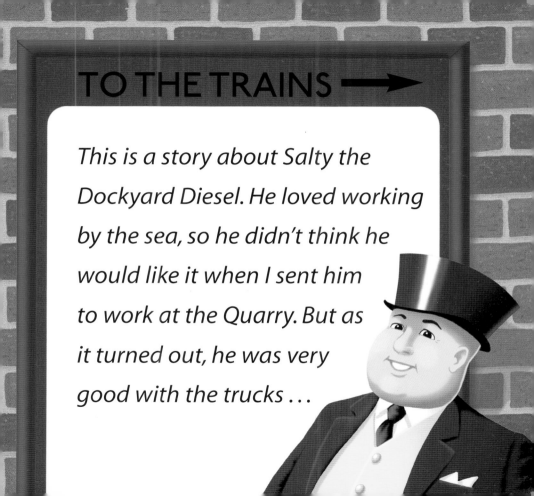

Salty was a dockyard diesel who loved telling tales about the sea.

One day, The Fat Controller asked him to come to the Island of Sodor to help finish an important job.

Salty was excited about working there because islands are surrounded by water, so he knew he would never be too far from the sea.

"Ahoy there, mateys!" said Salty when he arrived at his new job. "I'm here to help you."

"Welcome to Centre Island Quarry," said Mavis.

"A quarry?" said Salty in surprise. "But I'm a dockyard diesel! I'm used to working by the sea."

"You're a quarry diesel now," Mavis said.

Mavis explained that they had three days to complete The Fat Controller's important job. Salty was sad that he wasn't by the sea, but he was a Really Useful Engine, so he got started at once.

"Ah, well," he said. "At least I'll be working with trucks."

"You'd better watch them," said Mavis. "They can be rather tricky."

Bill and Ben, who were also working on the job, didn't think they needed any help – especially from a diesel!

"He won't last five minutes," said Bill.

"Yes, the trucks will trip him up soon enough," replied Ben.

But to their surprise, the trucks gave Salty no trouble at all.

"Yo, ho, ho and a bucket of prawns," Salty sang. "The tiller spins ..."

"... and the captain yawns," sang the trucks.

Thanks to Salty, by the end of the day the job was almost done. Bill and Ben were very surprised and rather jealous of Salty.

"Here comes Mister Show-off," Ben said when he saw Salty pulling a long line of trucks down the track.

"You have to admit he's got a knack with the trucks," said Mavis.

"Maybe, but Driver says he'll bore the bolts off us with his stories about the sea," huffed Bill.

That night, Salty didn't come into the engine shed. Mavis was worried. She rolled up next to him and asked him what he was doing outside.

"I thought I might catch a little sea breeze," said Salty sadly.

"You really do miss the sea, don't you?" said Mavis.

"Aye," sighed Salty. "I do."

Then Salty told Mavis some of his favourite stories about the sea.

Salty knew the quarry work was important, so the next day he told Bill and Ben his secret for getting the trucks to behave.

"I like working to a musical rhythm," he said. "And so do the trucks. Why don't you give it a try, me hearties?"

Bill and Ben thought singing songs sounded very easy. They decided to try it at once.

But Bill and Ben weren't very good at singing, and they couldn't remember the words of the songs!

Before long, the trucks were causing all sorts of trouble for them. Bill and Ben realised they would never be able to pull as many trucks as Salty. They watched jealously as Salty easily pulled long lines of trucks up and down the tracks.

Later that day, The Fat Controller came to the Quarry. He was surprised to see that his job had been finished.

"Well done!" he said to the engines. "You have worked very hard indeed!"

"We could never have done it without Salty," said Mavis.

Even Bill and Ben had to admit that Salty had helped them finish the job really quickly.

"Now I've got an even bigger job for you, Salty," said The Fat Controller.

"Aye, aye, Sir," said Salty sadly. "What kind of quarry is it this time?"

"Quarry?" said The Fat Controller. "I'm not sending you to a quarry. I want you to work at Brendam Docks!"

"The Docks are right by the sea!" said Salty excitedly.

"Yes, I thought you would like working there," replied The Fat Controller with a smile.

"Oh, thank you, Sir!" said Salty. "Now this reminds me of a time at the Harbour …"

And Salty was happily telling sea stories again.

Salty is still working at Brendam Docks. He is very happy there because he can smell the sea air and watch all the ships sailing past.

The engines on the Sodor Railway love working with Salty and they all admire the fact that he can pull more trucks than any three other engines put together!

The Thomas Story Library is THE definitive collection of stories about Thomas and ALL his friends.

5 more Thomas Story Library titles will be chuffing into your local bookshop in August 2008!

Jeremy
Hector
BoCo
Billy
Whiff

And there are even more Thomas Story Library books to follow late

So go on, start your Thomas Story Library NOW!

A Fantastic Offer for Thomas the Tank Engine Fans!

In every Thomas Story Library book like this one, you will find a special token. Collect 6 Thomas tokens and we will send you a brilliant Thomas poster, and a double-sided bedroom door hanger! Simply tape a £1 coin in the space above, and fill out the form overleaf.

TO BE COMPLETED BY AN ADULT

To apply for this great offer, ask an adult to complete the coupon below
and send it with a pound coin and 6 tokens, to:
THOMAS OFFERS, PO BOX 715, HORSHAM RH12 5WG

☐ Please send a Thomas poster and door hanger. I enclose 6 tokens
plus a £1 coin. (Price includes P&P)

Fan's name..

Address...

....Postcode............................

Date of birth...

Name of parent/guardian..

Signature of parent/guardian..

Please allow 28 days for delivery. Offer is only available while stocks last. We reserve the right to change
the terms of this offer at any time and we offer a 14 day money back guarantee. This does not affect your
statutory rights.

☐ Data Protection Act: If you do not wish to receive other similar offers from us or companies we
recommend, please tick this box. Offers apply to UK only.